A CASE
for LIFE

A CASE for LIFE
Copyright © 2023 by Vincent Piccone

Published in the United States of America
ISBN   Paperback: 979-8-89091-003-5
ISBN   eBook: 979-8-89091-004-2

All rights reserved. No part of this publication may be reproduced, stored in a retrieval system or transmitted in any way by any means, electronic, mechanical, photocopy, recording or otherwise without the prior permission of the author except as provided by USA copyright law.

The opinions expressed by the author are not necessarily those of ReadersMagnet, LLC.

ReadersMagnet, LLC
10620 Treena Street, Suite 230 | San Diego, California, 92131 USA
1.619. 354. 2643 | www.readersmagnet.com

Book design copyright © 2023 by ReadersMagnet, LLC. All rights reserved.

Cover design by Ericka Obando
Interior design by Daniel Lopez

A CASE *for* LIFE

by VINCENT A. PICCONE, M.D.

ReadersMagnet, LLC

INTRODUCTION

Every person who lives on the face of the planet was conceived and made in the image of God. Therefore every person is of infinite value in God's sight. God loves all his created men and women when they are made. Every person conceived in the womb is a marvelously unique, one of a kind creation, that never existed before and will never exist again. God adds that there is a purpose to every human life.

God gave men and women reproductive capacity so that they may generate offspring like themselves but also very different. To these children are also given reproductive capacity so that the chain of life continues. There has been a continuous chain of human life since Adam and Eve. Individuals give rise to cities and cities to nations. There is remarkable diversity among the human family so that while all are part of the same human race all are different in their own ways and manner.

It is the teaching of the Catholic church that all life should be protected from the time of conception to the time of natural death. All men are given freedom of thought and action for as long as they live, as creatures of free will and thought. Human life must have dignity and respect. As life starts at conception so must human life be protected at that stage. Human embryonic and fetal development must also be protected as this is a vulnerable stage of life and is a necessity for any future existence as a infant child and man or woman.

There is and always has been a culture of death that starkly contrasts with a culture of life. The culture of death proposes a dark nihilistic existentialistic view of man. Men and women are given choice to end life in the womb as they see fit. Man becomes God and is given the power over life and death. This is conducted through abortion, birth control pills, and abortifacient drugs. Practically on the basis of whim or capriciousness human life can be destroyed and discarded. Legal abortion then, an intrinsic part of the culture of death, allows man to destroy in direct opposition to the commandment to man that he shall not kill

This book tries to explain a culture of life and why it is so important for men to value pregnancies and human life. It tries to make a case for life. The book, in addition to the abortion debate, tries to explain end of life issues in the chronically ill, and the sick, and the elderly, and the dying. It tries to make a case then the disabled, the genetically challenged, and the imperfect are just as important to human society as the healthy, the young.

The key to healthy societies is a succession of generations living in harmony who aid one another in the struggles of life. The young are taught and supported by the old who in term support the old when they need care and support. A society that devours its young though abortion is unhealthy and bound for death. While a society that celebrates life will prosper and multiply.

BIBLE PASSAGES

The are several passages in the bible that speak of the infant in the womb. Luke 1-39- "During those days Mary set out and traveled to the hill country in haste to a town of Judah, where she entered the house of Zechariah and greeted Elizabeth. When Elizabeth heard Mary's greeting , the infant leaped in her womb, and Elizabeth, filled with the holy spirit, cried out in a loud voice, and said, "Most blessed are you among women, and blessed is the fruit of your womb. And how does this happen to me, that the mother of my Lord should come to me? For at the moment the sound of your greeting reached my ears, the infant in my womb leaped for joy. Blessed are you who believed that what was spoken to you by the Lord would be fulfilled." This biblical passage speaks of the awareness of the infant in the womb and the ability of the infant to react to its surroundings.

In the book of Jeremiah (Jeremiah 1:5) it states " Before I formed you in the womb I knew you, before you were born I dedicated you, a prophet to the nations I appointed you." This passage would suggest that there is a purpose to every baby who is formed in its mother's womb, and that there is a purpose in God's eye for every baby he forms in the womb.

The book of Psalms (Psalm 139:13) states "You formed my in most being, you knot me I my mother's womb. I praise you, so wonderfully you made me; wonderful are your works. My very self you knew; my bones were not hidden from you, When I was being made in secret, fashioned as in the depths of the earth. You eyes foresaw my actions; in your book all were written down; my days were shaped, before one came to be." This portion of the psalm speaks of the beauty of God's creation in the womb and how God intends for life to exist in the world and that God has a place for each one of us.

With all man's science and knowledge he is still unable to create human life. In fact human life in is creation may be considered a miracle. It is different from all other life in that is made in the image and likeness of God. When human life is purposely destroyed we destroy the reflection of God in our world. Something is lost forever which cannot ever be replaced. The author believes that every unique human creation is made with a specific purpose and plan and that if we destroy this life we bring disaster upon ourselves.

All the bible passages speak of the sanctity of human life and the respect we must have for it. God creates human life and it is not the role of man to interfere in its course from the time of conception. There are times however when god sanctions the destruction of human life as he did in the case of David when the child born to David and Bathsheba died. Here the baby was born alive and God allowed the child to die even though David desperately wanted it to live. It is God who should control the destiny of life not man.

When we stop obeying God and fearing him we put ourselves in danger. Then it is God with his prerogative to destroy. He will rip the infant from their mother's wombs.

IN THE IMAGE OF GOD

Every person that is conceived in the womb is made in the image of God. Their personality reflects God's Glory, as do their strengths, their abilities, and their talents. To destroy human life before its natural death is to destroy someone made in the image of God.

IT TAKES A VILLAGE

There are so many infants unwanted before they are born. To change this fact the culture must be changed. People must come to value children. Children must be viewed as the next generation of people and cared for properly. Society in general must change. Unborn babies are somebody's children, grandchildren, nieces, nephews, brothers and sisters.

So much money is spent on the old. Why not some for the babies and young? People must be willing to care for children; and not just the parents. To change the culture to one of life, neighbors, the old and the, family must be adapted to help pregnant women and those women who care for the young. Many people are required to properly rear children and make them productive members of society.

To many people, babies, and children in general are a threat. They take resources; they expose our mortality, and of course they might replace us in our jobs. When Jesus was born and heralded as the newborn king of the Jews, King Herod sought to kill him. He had slaughtered all the children in a specific age range so he would be sure to kill Jesus. Children are a threat to our concepts of time, money, and control. They usurp our time and our money.

On the other hand, few people view children as our salvation. That they might care for us in our infirmity or old age, and as people who might care for us as we cared for them.

Then too we may have enemies who might consider our offspring as threats to them. They convince us as wolves in sheep's clothing to destroy our children as our lives may be simpler, wealthier, or more enjoyable. If our enemies succeed to convince us that it is better if we destroy our children, then there is no future, and we lose everything. In our secular, humanistic society where pleasure and entertainment are all that matters, children are unwanted. These people who hold these values are replaced with those who do see a future and seize it. Then too there are many despondent people who think the future bleak and not a place to raise children. These people have lost hope and lose their destiny and their children through despair.

Strong, vibrant cultures have at least a number of children to replace that culture or civilization, and perhaps even more for growth. Dying cultures have insufficient children to replace the population and little respect for infants and children. It interesting statement was once made that a baby is God's way of stating the world should go on.

Infants and children are a critical component to any society and societies that do not have infants and children die off rapidly.

A society that glamorizes sexual pleasure without procreation buys a lie and misunderstands the who purpose of male and female sexuality- to have children.

THE PRO-LIFE MOVEMENT

The pro-life movement in the United States has existed as long as legalized abortion and has had earlier roots. The pro-life movement seeks to overturn the infamous Roe v. Wade decision, establish a life at conception act, picket and shut down abortion clinics, provide alternatives for women who seek abortions, place in office, legislators, judges, and executives at the state and federal level who are pro-life, publicize the pain and suffering caused by abortion, stop federal and state funding of abortions, and neutralize the corrosive effects of planned parenthood, NARAL and other pro-abortion groups.

The pro-life movement is a broad collection of many different people and groups that have as their aim the elimination of legal abortion, a great decrease in the number of illegal abortions, and introduction of a culture of life. Some of these people know firsthand the tragedy of abortion and wish to stop the holocaust. Others, intrinsically understand the value of all human life and support means to stop abortion.

Many pro-life people have been vilified as extremists who have harassed women outside abortion clinics, threatened peoples lives, shot and killed doctors who perform abortions, or bombed abortion clinic or destroyed abortion clinic property. While their have been some pro-life people who probably have done some of these things out of frustration over the problem, there remains a question of whether some pro-choice people or institutions may have done these things to tarnish the image and validity of the pro-life movement. Certainly the assassination of doctors who perform abortions just before justices are selected to the United States Supreme Court is unusual. Most pro-life people are good citizens who peaceable express their concern over the abortion problem. They undoubtedly feel that the murder of sixty-million unborn children is extreme.

Pro-life people are active politically in that they vote pro-life candidates into office, form political action committees, attend the annual March for life in Washington, DC, peaceably picket outside abortion clinics, collect clothes and other baby and child goods for mothers who cannot afford them, support mothers who have elected to bear their children, meet as groups in Churches and clubs, to find solutions to the abortion problem, and probably most important- they pray for abortion to end.

Because abortion is so controversial and engenders so much hatred from people who sponsor and condone abortion, the pro-life activist is often ostracized and suffers persecution. People who speak out against abortion can lose jobs, be harassed by police, be declared insane and institutionalized, and be publicly targeted in the community. Abortionists on the other hand are often regarded as friends of women who are relieved of their "inconveniences", "solve" population problems, and remove "responsibilities" from men.

There is little financial reward to be pro-life and the rewards are often heaven directed. Pro-life people disparage over the millions of dollars made by abortion doctors, Clinics and hospitals to claim and destroy innocent human life.

SO YOU ARE PREGNANT

There are many circumstances where a woman might fear a pregnancy. The teenager who finds herself pregnant and alone or a mother who has many children and cannot afford another child. What is someone to do?

A teenager can go to a nearby crisis pregnancy center and ask for help. Some centers provide resources like clothing and baby clothes and emotional support. Some centers can also arrange for labor and delivery services for a new mother. Perhaps the mother is overwhelmed and cannot take care of a child. Adoption referrals can be made.

TO STOP ABORTION

Abortion is a difficult problem, raises many issues, and has become extremely politicized. The abortion problem must be solved on a personal basis, a societal basis, and a government basis.

Ideally, sexual intercourse between a man and woman would occur in marriage where children are wanted and procreation takes place. Unmarried teenagers often become pregnant and this can result in out of wedlock births. Support of the mother is often necessary as she is unable to support herself. Government support of unwed mothers may result in a decreased abortion rate. Adoption or support by family members are other alternatives. In large families whose resources are strained, help from family members can often help and government support may be helpful.

Large families produce children different from the standard nuclear family or families with one child. Children produced by rape or incest can be put up for adoption or raised by other members of the family or even the woman herself.

Training in children that stresses abstinence from sexual activity until one is mature enough to raise and support children is the best defense against high abortion numbers and rates.

On a societal level people in churches and synagogues can help people with unplanned pregnancies care for children. They can also stress the importance and value of human life. To donate time, money, clothes and other baby goods, and plain old emotional support can help many people and their babies. Infants must be supported through adulthood and so must the societal support continue.

At the governmental level, laws should be put in place to help support the defense of life. A life at conception act in congress would effectively gut the Roe V. Wade decision as it would define life as beginning with conception. Direct reversal of Roe v. Wade through choice of more conservative judges is also a possibility. Government programs that support pregnant women , their infants, and their children might also be beneficial.

To really overturn the abortion problem however must result in a complete transformation of society and its values. Society must encourage a culture of life and come to appreciate children and babies. Sexual activity and pleasure must be taken in the context that this is for procreation and the procreation of a new generation of children. Unless people see value in children and families civilization will collapse.

The stoppage of the abortion culture inevitably begins with the family. Children must feel that they are wanted and loved and that they have value. This concern for them will be manifested in a next generation that also values and respects children.

Every infant and child should be viewed as a gift from God; a unique creation made in the image of God who as special talents to help the world continue.

ADOPTION

An unmarried or married woman might be presented with circumstances that may make it almost impossible for her to keep her child. In such cases a close family relative such as a mother or grandmother might be interested to raise the child. Sometimes a friend may be able to take the infant and raise them. If this also is not possible then adoption may be a possible option.

Adoption presents many challenges to both the birth parents and the adoptive parents. While a child is taken from the natural parents the maternal infant bonds which formed first in the womb are disrupted. The natural mother's care and affection for the infant can never be fully replaced. Hereditary, cultural, medical histories may be different.

Between the adoptive and natural parents. The infant may also be of a different temperament than the adoptive family as opposed to the natural parents. Other factors may include use of drugs or alcohol by the natural mother.

Adoption on the other hand may provide an infant with a stable home atmosphere.

People who are interested and motivated to nurture the infant and give love are the best people to leave a child in the company of the company. It would be ideal if governments could help support unwed mothers or mothers with too many children. Financial support is very important to mothers who would otherwise be unable to support their children. To leave monies to adoptive parents would allow them to support their adoptive children.

Eventually most infants grow to adulthood and may want to meet their natural parents. Too often the adoptive parents feel uncomfortable with this as sometimes do the natural parents. Mechanisms should be set up in society to that adults can meet their natural parents and form relationships with them.

Children are wonderful creations and can provide warm family life to people who would otherwise be unable to have children in their families. Children in adoptive families can interact with other children in the family and learn good social skills, learn the meaning of love, and be cared for by people who have their interest at heart.

While many societies allow homosexual couples to adopt children this is a bad idea from a biblical point of view. Homosexuality is an abomination in the sight of God and children raised in such "families" may be exposed to perverse relationships and perverse behaviors. They are not healthy relationships and children should not be raised in them.

While the number of families and adults that want to raise children through adoption is less than the potential number of children that could be adopted one would hope that with proper societal structure in place that many more people would want to adopt.

Society and government should foster adoption as a vastly better alternative to other choices and make adoption to healthy stable couples easy and manageable.

THE CATHOLIC CHURCH AND ABORTION

Abortion is defined by the church as the intentional removal of the fetus from the womb before it is capable of living outside the uterus. Direct abortion is considered by the church to be a grievous sin comparable to homicide, since a fetus is considered to be a living human being.

In the United States, approximately fifty percent of women in the Catholic church have had abortions which emphasizes the magnitude of the abortion problem. Abortion in Europe, the United States, and elsewhere has caused growth of Church membership to slow, and in many areas to decrease. As a percentage of world population it is possible Catholic church membership has fallen compared to Muslim, Chinese, and hindu populations.

Abortion is considered to be a mortal sin by the Catholic church, so members should refrain from further abortions and seek aid in the confessional. Abortion puts a woman or man involved in the process at risk of hellfire.

The church provides services to aid women in giving birth to their children instead of abortion. Sometimes the church will provide, food, clothing, shelter, and healthcare to pregnant women. The Sisters of Life are a Catholic group of religious nuns who have dedicated their lives to help solve the abortion problem. Priests for Life is a group of Catholic Priests and lay people who are also committed to help stop the abortion dilemma. The Sisters of life and Priests for life are committed to help women recover from the trauma of abortion. Project Rachel is another group who help women from the misery of abortion and recover from the post traumatic syndrome caused by abortion.

Pope John Paul II spoke of the Culture of Life and how it must be established in the Western world for it to survive. Mother Theresa also spoke of the destructive effects caused by the destruction of the maternal-infant bond seen in cultures with abortion. People who have suffered abortion often initially fall away from the Church and it is the interest of all concerned to see these people reunited with the church.

The Catholic Church, the universal church, the legacy of Jesus must truly be committed to see the eradication of abortion. The wanton and widespread destruction of human life is in direct contradiction to the Gospel of Jesus Christ about the Sanctity and preciousness of human life.

All churches that claim to be Christian should also encourage an end to abortion. More generally, there have been close to two billion abortions in the world, to include other cultures, over the last forty years. Abortion is divisive, an act of killing, and akin to warfare. There can be no peace in the human family when abortion is widespread and pervasive as it is.

The catholic faith has been constantly attacked by its stand on abortion but no other institution on earth has consistently maintained the dignity and value of the unborn infant.

THE DIABOLICAL

Legalized abortion is satanic. Court judgments or laws which suggest that it is alright to abort an unborn baby are evil. These decisions and laws have an effect to erode the conscious' of women and erode the values of societies. One of the most basic bonds in society is that between the mother and the child and abortion destroys this bond as it destroys the unborn infant. Legalized abortion is the work of the devil and his lies. It is never justifies to kill someone and that is what abortion does. The abortion industry however lies about what actually takes place.

Abortion separates man from woman and causes discord between the two. Where love is supposed to be-it is replaced by hatred and anger. The devil brought death into the world and abortion is death. Legalized abortion causes people to sin and this separates people from God, a primary goal of the devil. Abortion divides people. The abortion industry represents that the handicapped, down's children, people with certain hereditary diseases, the poor, those with too large families should all have abortions. Infants made in the image and likeness of God should be aborted- this too is diabolical.

The abortion industry and abortionists represent that it is alright to practice fornication and adultery and that these practices are without consequence Teenagers are encouraged to have intercourse outside of marriage as it is pleasurable. Little do they understand the magnitude of their folly.

Abortion is a sin against the person, the mother, and against the soul. The mother sins by destroying her unborn infant. It is a sin which tears at the soul and destroys the person. It destroys the soul as it replaces good with evil, happiness and joy with sadness and mourning, life with death, light with darkness, and heaven with hell. Abortion destroys friendship when women seek counsel from their most intimate acquaintances that a pregnancy should be ended. With the diabolical promises and assurances that life can be tidied and sanitized through the death of an unwanted infant comes unrest and anxiety the opposite of peace and security a woman might want.

Few things are more diabolical and demonic that legalized abortion. It tears at the social and political fabric to leave society in ruins. The only antidote is confession, repentance, and prayer. The devil and demons will only be pushed aside and out of civilization when people come to realize how destructive abortion really is. The "right" and "choice" and "liberty" of abortion are as fruit of the tree of knowledge of good and evil in Eden and should never be eaten.

Racism, class warfare, radical feminism, intergenerational warfare, humanism, and sexual warfare are all the deadly fruits of the abortion industry. There can be no peace with widespread legalized abortion. God tolerates abortion as much as he tolerates the devil and the demons- temporarily. The devil wants lots of company in hell, and legalized abortion presents lots of opportunity for people to join him. When people choose abortion they choose the Satanic. One prays that they turn their hearts toward God before it is too late.

DIVERSITY

Every pregnancy, every child conceived, is a new creation. When many different couples have children, all these people created are different-there is genetic diversity. Attempts to eliminate the poor, or the physically handicapped, or the mentally retarded, or the genetically challenged limit the size of the gene pool, and make the population less able to adapt to genetic pressures. For example of the population of sickle cell diseased is eliminated then the population will be less able to resist malaria.

A SPARK OF LIFE

It all started with Adam. God took clay made it in the form of man and breathed life into the clay. The man became alive with a spark of life. Woman was made from Adam's rib which God built up, a second spark of life. Ever since there has been a transmission of those original sparks of life to succeeding generations. The cycle of birth and death has repeated itself hundreds of times since the dawn of creation, each birth initiated by a spark of life. Despite all man's technology and know how he has not been able to duplicate that spark of life.

Once sperm and egg meet- automatically a new human life is created that is a distinct and unique creation. Even identical twins or clones do not share the exact same characteristics. When the cells of that newly created life begin to divide and multiply and come to share the characteristics of the human form the heart beats and the brain begins to exhibit electric waves. That life if protected and nurtured will be born as an infant and grow into childhood.

Human life necessarily is quite different from the inanimate. It grows, it wakes, it sleeps, and it moves. Its image is quite different from that of all other things-It is made in the image of God. Human conception gives rise to both the male and the female of the species. It is the female that is given the opportunity to bear and raise children when she is mature.

New human life makes itself known early to the mother. Monthly periods cease. Later she can feel movement of the infant in her body.

THE CULTURE OF LIFE

The culture of life is one that protects human life from the moment of conception to the time of natural death. A culture of life recognizes the genius of the divine creator to create human life out of the inanimate, that God creates new life for a purpose, and that human life is divinely inspired and in the image of God. The culture of life recognizes God and that human beings are not God.

The culture of life makes no judgment on the value of human life and does not place a value on any individuals head or life. A culture of life acknowledges the right of the individual to food, water, clothing and other basic necessities of life and of the right of individuals to seek and receive love, affection, and other emotional support. The culture of life recognizes the right to life and its core foundation for all other rights.

The culture of life recognizes a continuum of life from conception to death with interspersed periods and times of growth and that no-one has the right to terminate or destroy except for those times allowed by the creator of that life because of the self –will of that individual to choose self chosen evils to God, the society, or himself.

The culture of life asserts the value, the dignity, and the importance of any given life; recognizes that life starts in the woman's body and is temporarily a part of the woman's body though distinct from it. The culture of life recognizes the procreative force of man and the responsibility of couples to exercise their reproductive capacities with wisdom and discipline.

CRIME STATISTICS

As the 1990's started people who tracked crime statistics noticed that the crime rate began to fall. Murder, rape, burglary, and other crime rates began to decrease. Apparently someone linked this to the Roe V. Wade decision and stated that the fall in crime rate was directly related to the start of Roe V. Wade in 1973 that "legalized" criminal abortion.

It is the understanding of the author that the rates were more significant in the African-American community- that decrease in crime rate was proportional to decreased relative birth rates in this population and relative increased rates of abortion in the United States. While the population was increased over the years that ensued the actual relative crime rate for many categories of crime decreased.

As important the rate of crime fell in poor communities and this also was linked to a higher abortion rate. Poor people commit more crime so if the percentage of the population that is poor decreases then the crime rate will decrease or so we are told. If only all the poor mother's aborted their babies then perhaps the crime rate could be decreased to zero.

Many factors might have accounted for the decreased crime rate but the abortion story for blacks and poor caught headlines. The poor and the African Americans accounted for more crime so that justifies abortion of their children.

Perhaps if abortion was again considered a crime it would have resulted in a higher crime rate. Of the sixty million abortions completed since 1973 through 2011 many women would have been imprisoned for destroying their unborn children and thousands of "doctors" would be jailed for criminal abortion. If the factors were included in crime statistics their would be added sixty million murders.

Perhaps many rape statistics were "fixed" prior to 1973. Women claimed rape in order to obtain a more legal abortion even though there had been no rape. Maybe there was left theft as poor people and African

Americans no longer had to steal to feed and clothe their children. Those children no longer existed. And perhaps the murder rate went down because because men and women no longer fought over their unborn child's welfare as their was no longer any welfare to fight over.

Perhaps the Roe v Wade decision resulted in lower crime statistics but not because of the fact that fewer criminals were conceived, but because their were obviously sixty million fewer people.

In any event there was much less need for courts, police officers, prisons, parole officers, prison guards and the tax payer could better afford to live especially those in the middle and upper classes. So much for the statement that the poor shall inherit the kingdom of God. With millions of less poor there was also less need for social services, social workers, subsidized housing, food stamps, and the like.

CONDOMS

A condom is a latex sheath that fits over the penis during sexual intercourse. It collects semen after ejaculation and protects against some venereal diseases.

There is great controversy today over the use of condoms. Many liberal groups insist that condom use be employed with teenagers today who seek to have sexual intercourse. The controversy is with more conservative groups who argue that condom use should not be taught to teenagers nor should condoms be supplied to teenagers.

Liberal groups insist that condoms would cut down the pregnancy rate in teenagers as semen would not be deposited in the vagina. The abortion rate would thus decrease to make a dent in the high abortion numbers. Conservative groups argue that the failure rate in condom use is high enough that there would still be a large number of abortions if the teenagers decided to end their pregnancies by abortion.

Christian groups and most notably Catholic theologians state that sexual intercourse should be between two people legally married to each other, that sexual intercourse is procreative and should be applied to conceive children, and that condom use with married couples is improper.

Fornication is defined as sexual intercourse between unmarried people. It is considered a sin by Christian groups most notably Catholics. According to the bible fornicators do not enter the kingdom of God and therefore are condemned to hell. Condom use in teenagers therefore effects the soul and when they are not married has grave effects on the person's future. The concept of fornication, God, and heaven and hell, are intricately intertwined in the condom debate. Those who do not believe in heaven and hell or God think there is nothing wrong with condoms whereas those who believe in God an heaven and hell believe that sexual intercourse between unmarried teenagers whether with a condom or not place their souls in grave danger.

The real conflict is over sexual abstinence in teenagers and others who are not married. Sexual abstinence and virginity until marriage protects against pregnancy and thus stops abortion. It also it would seem protects the soul. Is it possible that those who want to see teenagers use condoms and have sexual intercourse before marriage want to see these teenagers or their souls destroyed. To say it is alright for teenagers to have sex with condoms suggests it is alright for teenagers to have sex without condoms.

In addition to the abortion and pregnancy question is also a question of sexually transmitted diseases. The HIV-Aids virus and the hepatitis virus can often be transmitted through microscopic holes in the condoms. Condoms sometimes break which make the transmission of syphilis, gonorrhea, chlamidia, and other sexually transmitted diseases a distinct possibility.

Pleasure, another goal of sexual intercourse, is what teenagers want despite the risk to the soul, the body, and concern about pregnancy, and abortion.

FEMINISM AND ABORTION

Feminism may be defined as all that defends women's rights. A basic tenet of feminism is that woman have control over their bodies and that women have a right to abortion. This concept is flawed however in many respects. Of the 60,000,000 legal abortions in the United States between 1973 and 2011, 30,000,000 of this have involved girl infants. In defending the right to abortion, the feminists, have put to death, tens of millions of baby girls, denying the future women a basic right to life.

Control of a woman over her body appears limited to abortion however. Do women have a right to bear children? The law never explicitly states a woman has a right to conceive and bear a child nor do feminists argue for this right. Women, biologically, are the only members of society who can bear children. In a family, a woman has control over how many children are generated in the family, and the law denies men any say over how many children are generated.

Women are to have control over their bodies and can use birth control and sterilization as means of controlling the number of births. This is enshrined in the all-powerful right to privacy enshrined in federal court decisions. Imagine if all women exercised this right. There would be no next generation of people. Some women marry and bear children others do not. Some women bear children and others do not. It appears society picks out who will bear children and who will not.

Women may have less control over their bodies than they might choose. Many women exercise their right to bear children only until they are older. They then find out biologically that they are unable to have children because they have waited to long.

Women have control over their bodies but at what cost. With abortion they are at risk for death and injury. What right can protect a woman from death if her abortion goes awry? Or if the woman goes into shock or has bowel perforation, or bleeds to death.

Hundreds of women have died from legal abortions. What right protected these women? Some women become sterile after abortions. Who can restore their fertility?

If a woman is coerced by husband or boyfriend to have an abortion what choice does the woman have? Freedom or choice suggest alternatives that most women do not have and cannot exercise. The freedom of choice "exercised" by most women is merely a cover for coerced abortion by governments to achieve population control and meet government quotas for births so that planned population goals are met.

Does a woman have a right to bear a down's syndrome child or deformed child, or a child with a metabolic or genetic defect, or once again is she coerced to have an abortion to ensure genetic and "health" of the population? And does a woman have a choice when her employer says she will have to quit work when she is pregnant because the employer does not mean to expend benefit money for the pregnancy?

Have woman been duped into destroying their unborn children under a guise of choice?

PARENTAL NOTIFICATION

There are many laws in many States that make it acceptable for a minor to have an abortion without the knowledge of her parents. Minors are thought to have the judgment and experience to understand the risks of abortion and gravity of situation in which they are involved.

It might be questioned whether the possible risk of death or severe injury to include sepsis, severe hemorrhage, bowel perforation or permanent sterility is understood well by a sixteen year old, fifteen year old girl, or even younger female. Certainly the abortion lobby would like it both ways- that a underage female is mature enough to undergo a procedure with such grave consequences but not mature enough to raise a child with aid and support from a family. Apparently the abortion lobby is more interested in females having abortions than having children- it makes sense since abortion is their business.

The father may be another teenager or as is often the case a man in his thirties or forties. The question of statutory rape is raised when the girl is underage. The abortion may certainly protect the man from charges of statutory rape or even from child support. Rules that would protect children from statutory rape are often not followed. Demand for child support are rarely made. Society does not put pressure on these couple to marry but rather to have abortions. Again several centuries ago it was common practice for young girls to marry and have children, the life span was also much shorter. People would necessarily have to bear children when they were young before they died.

When should parents be informed that their children are pregnant are might face a decision to have an abortion. A frequent argument is made that a parental consent is required for a tonsillectomy or an appendectomy. Why not an abortion? Is the concept of privacy again invoked to include teenagers and abortion? Some parents first become aware that there child had an abortion when their child has been severely injured or even died after an abortion. The great majority of parents however never find out abort their child's abortion. One wonders whether the parents of a teenager might try and avoid an abortion if they realized that the infant destroyed was in fact their grandchild.

Of course many parents want no parental consent laws exactly because they know their children are pregnant and want them to have abortions without their express knowledge. It is probable that most parents want their children to have abortions if they become pregnant. This might because they do not want to support their child and grandchild, do not like the father of the child, or resent the stigma of their daughter as a single parent and teenager.

Abortionists sometimes state that abortion is safer than childbirth and that underage girls are nor prepared physically for childbirth. These arguments are self serving to those who perform abortions. The vast majority of teenagers who undergo deliveries suffer no adverse health issues and deliver health babies. Parents should know these facts when considering the destruction of their grandchildren.

PLANNED PARENTHOOD

Planned Parenthood is a non profit organization started by Margaret Sanger to help poor women with birth control so that they could have manageable families. Margaret Sanger believed that unless women in poor families had birth control that more children would be brought into the world than the family could manage. It is hard to decide which came first the large family or the poverty. Did poverty increase the size that a family would have or did large families produce poverty. It is almost as if Margaret Sanger thought that if your reduce the size that families have, especially poor ones, then you could eliminate poverty. The natural end of this argument is that if poor people do not have families then there will be no poverty.

With the advent of the birth control pill, family planning became practical. Women placed on birth control pills would not conceive children or their conceived children would not take root in the uterus. Women who did become pregnant would be able to have abortions. If the pill did not work then the back-up plan was to abort the children.

About the same time as Margaret Sanger, the government stepped in and gave financial aid to poor families. This replaced charitable giving from churches and others to the poor. There were strings attached, if a family received aide it would have to adhere to the policy that the government could determine family size. The government went into the business of regulating family size.

Planned parenthood has become the leading abortion provider in the United States performing over one hundred thousand abortion yearly. It has gone headlong into the abortion business. This stark fact has been softened by the fact that Planned Parenthood also provides services for birth control, venereal disease treatment, and well health care check ups.

The bible states that the poor shall inherit the earth. With the advent of planned parenthood it is the middleclass and the rich that inherit the kingdom of God. The rich were relieved of their obligation to support the poor and poor families. The government went into the abortion business by funding planned parenthood.

Planned parenthood has been so effective that the birth rate in the United States has actually declined. Immigration now accounts for most of the population increase. The sad fact is that a Christian country decreases its reputation and status in the world by badgering the poor to sterilize, birth control, and abort themselves out of existence.

Planned parenthood and those in power are committed to the two child family and do not for the most part want to see large families. The government is concerned about population grow in excess of what it thinks it can handle. The governments think that abortion and birth control can avoid famine, and pestilence, and war. Perhaps there will be more of the same if the governments continue on this course.

TOO MANY PEOPLE?

Malthus postulated that the multiplication of new people and a bigger population would continue until the number of people would exceed the food supply and that then there would be famine and disaster. There are many people today who think that there are too many people; that the world is overpopulated. Policy was put in place that families should be smaller and that less people should be born.

Pollution, the non-sustainable use of the earth's resources, lack of water and food-are all touted as reasons for there to be fewer people. In essence fewer people means fewer problems. People are rarely looked upon as solutions to the problem but rather as the problem.

Chances are we will never see people spread to other planets let alone other solar systems. We are then to remain on the planet called earth. By all predictions the planet can only hold maximum of thirty-six billion people. This figure could be achieved in only a couple of decades if populations are unchecked. What then is the ideal number of people to live on the earth. Who then is to have children and who is not to have children? Who will inherit the earth?

Policy decisions have been made that people should have smaller families. Two children is referred to as an ideal. But what about children who die before marriage, who are infertile, who die of cancer, who are homosexual, etc. For each family to have two children does not result in a steady population but one of decline. Family policy in Europe and the United States has already resulted in decline in the native populations. Some societies may find extinction of their populations if current trends continue.

Larger families consume more resources but have some benefits. Children but be better adjusted and be more agile. Larger families might produce more balanced children. For every one to have too children might be a solution demographically but might be a disaster socially.

People consume resources yet are also solutions. The same people who consumes resources may also plant trees, recycle raw materials, build affordable housing, plant crops, develop new energy sources and the like. Man can be productive or destructive,- it is his choice. To those who think people are assets the more people the better and to those who think of people as greedy consumers and polluters the more the worse off we are.

There are many people who believe that population should be controlled by controlling the number of babies who are born- to only allow a certain number of births independent of the number of pregnancies. Maybe on the other hand God wants all babies who are conceived to be born. It is then man who is defying the divine will. When we artificially limit the number of children born do we rely on our own understanding of life and the future and ignore God's.

When governments raise people like cattle and allow only a certain number of yearly live births to stabilize population they also may throw out love and family life.

THE ABORTION SNOWBALL

Since the Roe Verses Wade decision more and more men and women have had to deal with the ordeal of abortion. As more women have abortions the fact that they have destroyed their sons or daughters must become more sublimated if those people are to maintain their sanity. Abortion, to them, if they are initially negative or neutral about the option, must become acceptable if they are to rationalize their decisions. Thus every day legal abortion continues, the ranks of men and women who psychologically must see legal abortion continue, despite the reality of the evil that it is, increase. This is a difficult dynamic to reverse.

Women who have had abortions it would seem have also to recommend abortions to other women who face difficulties with their pregnancies. Abortion referral of a woman who has had an abortion to other women who have not had one makes it all the more acceptable to that woman who has already had one. This might explain why many women who have had abortions work in abortion clinic. It eases the consciences of women who have had abortions who work in abortion clinics to see other women undergo the procedure. If its alright for them it must also be alright for me when I had mine.

Men too have their consciences eased when other men take their wives or girlfriends for abortions. If every one is doing it, it must be alright- the herd mentality.

As more people suffer the pains of legal abortion there is also less willingness to change the law. If abortion is legal when I had my abortion, and the law in the future says that it is illegal, then I did something wrong and illegal. NO-body wants to have dome anything illegal so the law will have to stay the same. With social and government pressure for women to terminate pregnancies, a law that states that it is legal, and the large number of people already affected by abortion, the momentum is for this tragedy to continue well into the future.

People become numb to what abortion really is- the murder of innocents. To solve the abortion snowball will take the large majority of those not affected by abortion, the mass realization by those affected by abortion that there is something very wrong about this procedure, or a combination of the two. To really stop abortion will also involve necessarily the medical community. Doctors, nurses, and others in the abortion area will have to come to some collective realization about how destructive the abortion debacle is.

Politically, the abortion problem, is highly polarizing and has placed America, in two camps, those who favor abortion and those who don't. The argument goes further in that many politicians have personally been involved with abortion. One thinks sometimes, with the rancor of the arguments that anything short of a civil was, where the antiabortionists win, will not change the abortion dynamic to prolife. In one regard if abortion does destroy the country socially, economically, demographically, and politically, then the argument will be settled as the dust settles.

SOMETHING'S MISSING

With 80 million abortions since 1973 there is something missing in the United States. Quite possible this could be sixty million people. Men, women, infants, children, adolescents, middle aged people- all missing-gone forever. Artists, electricians, politicians, doctors, moms, pops, delicatessen owners, and a multitude of others. The youth of the country destroyed.

Churches, are emptier, schools are emptier, hospitals are emptier, towns and cities are emptier- everything is emptier. The economy is smaller and hell is fuller.

SICK MOMS TO BE

There are many diseases that can effect the pregnant woman and some of these are fatal. What happens to the pre-born infant in these cases? Must the infant be destroyed to protect the life of the mother?

While the number of women who might sacrifice their babies to save themselves compared to the 1.6 million abortions done each year in the United States, this, the rape issue, and the incest issue are constantly thrown in the face of the public to justify legal abortion. Almost all pregnancies are not the result of rape or incest, and almost none threatens the life of the mother.

A mother-to-be might be threatened with breast cancer, or cervical, or uterine cancer, eclampsia, or other diseases that can kill the mother. There might be no way to save the infant as the pregnancy might be early, and no treatment will save the mother because of the stage of the disease. In this case both mother and infant die. In some cases treatment can be delayed till the infant is born. In this case both mother and child can be saved. In a third scenario, the mother can only be saved by treatments, in a timely manner, that destroy the infant. In this case the mother must make a choice-either to forsake treatment, and let her baby live or, prioritize her life and sacrifice her infant.

The last situation is the most heartbreaking for a woman and her family. Some one must die! Especially if the woman's family is large and she has other children to care for. The drama is less when you realize that there might be no cure for the woman anyway and she might die soon afterward. Life is weighed in the balance and people must decide which life is more precious the infant's or the mother's. In another light one might ask whether the mother's love for her unborn child is so great that she would want to sacrifice her love for her infant after that of the love for her own life.

No-one would question if a mother drowned to save her drowning child or was killed by a bear to protect her child from the bear, but the infant has become much less precious when the infant is still in the mother's body. Indeed, the whole abortion industry and society in general devalues life in the womb as disposable. It is a rare woman who believes the life in her womb is as precious as a infant, child, or person outside the womb.

In essence the question is which life is more precious-that of the mother, or that of the infant in the mothers womb. The answer should be that both are equally important and the greatest effort should be made to save both lives. Life is important. If the mother must choose between her life and that of her child, that decision should be left up to the mother, and her physician. No one would call her selfish if she sacrifices her infants life for that of her own, and only few would call her a saint if she sacrifices her life for that of her child.

The decision is even more heartbreaking when the infant is the mother's first child, and she may not live ling enough to bear more children. The future generations of her family depend on the woman's decision about her pregnancy.

SICK BABIES

Most babies are born healthy and become individuals who live an extended lifespan. There are babies however who are born sick or have hereditary diseases that start in the womb. Some people believe that it is better for the baby not to be born. There are however many reasons why a pregnancy should be allowed to carry to term.

A fetus or infant in the womb is made in the image and likeness of God- a unique creation. To not allow a baby to be born is to destroy God's work. God, the author and finisher of life should be the only one to say when someone's life should finish. When we take someone's life because we believe that their will be suffering or that there will be no quality of life we make judgments that are not proper. God may have a reason for a sick baby to be born, a reason that maybe only he knows.

Some people state that it is to expensive to take care of sick babies, yet hundreds of billions of dollars are spent each year on the elderly who may live only a short time. Judgments are made that only one stage of life should be supported. These judgments are wrong. How ill people ever learn to take care of sick babies unless some are born. Medicine will never advance unless people learn to take sick babies and either prevent disease or cure it.

Parents and families suffer when sick babies are born. The suffering helps build a bond between the parents and the infant even if the infants life is short. The bond can help strengthen family ties and make for a better family.The suffering can also become a offering to God from the family. No one wants a sick baby but one who is healthy and sick babies put into perspective the great gift God gives when a healthy baby is born. Sick babies also make us grateful to God for our own health.

In the Christian faith people believe that souls are given when a infant is conceived and that soul is immortal. Who are we then to interfere in the natural course of someone's life no matter how sick they are? Euthanasia presents the same problems. Man is not wise enough nor empowered to terminate someone's life before that persons natural time for death.

Eugenics a process where those who are considered unfit are destroyed before they are born and other methods of selection of those who are considered more fit allows man to play God a job he is not very good at.

In the book if second Samuel in the bible, King David Sins. He sleeps with Bathsheba, the wife of someone else. Bathsheba conceives a child. The child becomes gravely ill and eventually dies. The childs illness is caused by the parents sin. Sickness in a child may be a result of the sins of the parents. A sick child can bring us to terms with our own sin and make us repent. How often is HIV-AIDS in an infant caused by the sins of the parents. Congenital syphilis is another example.

Sick children can sometimes be caused by a genetic disease. Counsel with a geneticist can sometimes prevent illness is our children and help us find healthy children.

A BITTER PILL TO SWALLOW

A new abortion pill was created in the late 1980's called RU-486. It is the understanding of the author of this book that the pill causes abortion as it causes separation of the placenta from the uterine wall. The baby is no longer supplied with oxygen or nutrients from the mother and promptly dies. Another drug, a prostaglandin is administered so that the dead infant is expelled from the mother's body.

RU-486, the abortion pill, has allowed expectant mother's to kill their baby, without the necessity of a surgical abortion, and without the services of a physician. The do it yourself, at home abortion can be done cheaply, effectively, and in the comfort on one's home. It is truly a private matter between a woman and her god.

What are the consequences of the pill? Most chemical abortions are done by physicians who order and supply the drug. Abortion statistics can still be kept by the government for their use. Women have died from the drugs mostly because of bleeding, although death from other causes have occurred. Many women bleed heavily and require transfusion.

Perhaps psychologically the drug may be difficult to bear as the dead infant is passed into the toilet or a basin. The mother then realizes the full results of her act unlike a surgical abortion. The mother sees for herself that it is a unborn infant and not just tissue. Perhaps it is the realization that new human life can be snuffed out only by taking a pill. Then there is the possibility one day that the drugs which may be injected can be used for involuntary abortion.

Are not pills meant to salvage, restore, and heal life and not to destroy it. The pill when ordered by a physician destroys life in direct violation of the Hippocratic oath, and the whole history of medicine. Abortion makes the doctor the murderer in stead of the healer he is meant to be.

In the catholic faith, the birth control pill is also thought evil because it otherwise prevents the fertilized egg from implanting in the woman's body. The fertilized egg can be defined as new human life. An entity that will never again exist if it is destroyed. RU-486 also destroys unique human life made in the image and likeness of God.

The abortion pill makes abortion easy- too easy! It denigrates the concept and value of life, and makes human life disposable and value less. One wonders if it does not make woman callous when life can be destroyed so easily.

To go one step further, does not the abortion pill, make women gods who can create and destroy life at will. Does this pill replace the real God and his judgments and values with a woman's conscience. Is it man's place to take human life and make decisions as to what is wanted, valuable, and valid, and that which is not? Perhaps they should call it the god pill rather than the abortion pill. When life is reduced to relative utilities, we should be afraid because our lives can be judged on the same basis.

ROE VERSUS WADE

The 1973 supreme court decision took the criminal act of abortion and make abortion respectable. What had previously been considered a crime was now legal. To change the law meant a change in values, a change in behavior, and a change in punishment. The trimesters of pregnancy were used by the legal profession to define when the unborn child could legally be destroyed. It imposed grave new rules on the medical profession that stated the Hippocratic oath was no longer in fashion- (which stated that a physician should not perform an abortion on a woman.) The medical profession was obligated by reason of the law to perform abortions on women for essentially any reason. Furthermore the Roe V. Wade decision and other privacy decisions by courts stripped the father of any rights and made the progress of pregnancy to birth or its termination beforehand a decision exclusive to the mother.

The decision of a law court which consisted of nine judges would forever change the way a nation would view the human person in the womb.

BABIES OF RAPE

There are two cases of rape in the bible. In the first case Dinah is raped by a man from another culture who found her very attractive and had indeed fallen deeply in love with her. His family offers to have the young man marry her but Jacob's sons, angry that their sister had been violated kill all the males of the foreign tribe. The rape caused much trouble for Dinah and her family. In the second case Tamar is raped by her step brother. This two causes grave circumstances for all concerned.

There are thousands of cases of rape each year in the United States. There are more cases all around the world. In a fraction of these cases of rape.

SEEING OURSELVES IN OUR CHILDREN

When we have children, the generations continue, the DNA propagates, and the chain of life extends into the future. If every person makes a positive contribution to the world, then this chain of life is important.

TWO BODIES

When a woman becomes pregnant there are two people; one new and one older. There is a new individual growing inside her. This new person is very different from her but at the same time shows much similarity to her. This new individual is not just tissue but a complete DNA model different from the mother's DNA model. While the DNA is different it came in part from exactly half from the mother's DNA.

The cry of the women's liberty and freedom groups is that the woman has a right to terminate this new individual because it is her body and she should have control over it. When a woman has sexual intercourse however she must accept that there is a chance she should become pregnant and that an new individual might be created. While society has not accepted that this individual has rights, the fact remains that a new special individual has been created. Women's liberation denies the humanity of the new life. A new life despite this fact has been created.

Women, especially single women, do have control over their bodies. They can refuse to engage in sexual intercourse. Teenagers and older women implicitly realize that a new life might be created by the sexual act. This has been taught by the family and society. Sexuality that results in pregnancy is the choice of two people but those two people make a third person. To state that a woman should have control over her body after a pregnancy results does do impugn the humanity of the newly created life nor does validate any control which seeks to terminate that new life.

Sex is pleasurable and to some, fun. It is however no game. Sex despite all the birth control pills and societal view that this is a recreation still can result in the production or reproduction of new individuals. Babies are formed in the woman's body- some times one and frequently more.

To give complete control to the woman over the new life that is generated or to give that control to man, or society in general denies the humanity of the new life. More importantly when control over life is given to third parties, the mother and father in particular, relinquishes control that those same people have over themselves. This is to say that if people destroy the fetus because they have control over their bodies puts them a risk of someone to say that people can lose control over their own bodies. If the humanity of the fetus is denied, then the humanity of any individual on the planet is threatened. When the unborn life can be negated then all of our lives are in danger.

When people seek control over other people's bodies they in fact lose control over their own. Women do have complete control over their bodies, even to the point of suicide. With abortion pills, self-help literature to perform abortions on themselves, and the ever-present possibility that a woman can find someone to abort her, there is absolute control over one's body. This does not eliminate the fact that a new life has been generated nor does it destroy the rights of the unborn baby. With choice comes the possibility of death both to the unborn baby and the mother herself.

WHEN GOD ACTS

Many people believe that abortion is a woman's choice, a woman's freedom, and a woman's right. Some women might not feel this ways when their family or boyfriend pushes them into a abortion clinic. Some women might not feel this way when their boss, who may have to give them benefits threatens them with job dismissal if they do not abort their baby. Some might not feel this way when there are denied basic rights to food water, and shelter when they are pregnant. Some might not feel this way if a government thinks that there are too many births and some women need to abort.

Then too-there is God. When a person or group of people turn away from God, then God can punish those people through abortion or forms of it. The prophets spoke of women being cut open and their babies destroyed when they forsake God. And even Jesus spoke of women losing their unborn children when they did not realize the time of their visitation. God demands exclusive allegiance and when we drift away from his we risk his wrath. God gives children to the humble, the lowly, and the poor and those who worship him. Indeed the meek and the poor shall inherit the earth. In a society that is secular and humanistic and everything goes, children are not valued and God destroys that culture, or should one say, God lets them destroys themselves.

Then too- God causes women to miscarry or have abortions. While not all woman who miscarry are adulterers or fornicators, there is a high incidence of miscarriage in this group.

Perhaps the high abortion rate in the world is due to people who prioritize pleasure and sexuality for the sake of it over children and infants. When people watch pornography and pornographic movies rather than go to church or synagogue they have lost God's sense of what sexuality is all about- to bear and raise children. The abortion industry makes it clear that people are entitled to sexuality and birth control so that they can enjoy their sexuality without benefit of children. When a child is conceived then it is just a nuisance and a birth control failure that must result in abortion.

Sexuality and children were Gods gift to man. When sexuality is misused God lets people destroy themselves and their children through abortion. God intended man and woman to marry and use their sexuality to bear children to form families and propagate and continue the species. Not to lustfully engage other people's wives. While single motherhood is not the ideal and a very difficult choice, perhaps many single pregnant women abort their children because they were only interested in indulging their sexuality.

God causes some miscarriage and natural abortion and has his own reasons for doing so which are out of mans knowledge. Why do not people let pregnancies carry to term when God wants then to and man not interfere by performing abortions that are unnecessary and contrary to God's will. God is the author and finisher of life. Let him decide when life should be terminated. When man plays God the world is in great peril. Man, and especially doctors, do not have God's wisdom, and when they interfere with the natural course and trajectory of life they can sometimes destroy God's creation.

IN VITRO FERTILIZATION

In a relatively new process, eggs are removed from the woman's belly and put in a petri dish. Sperm are added to the dish and the eggs are fertilized. The fertilized eggs are then placed in the woman's uterus where some may implant.

The process does not involve sexual intercourse between a man and a woman. Eggs can be taken from any woman and sperm from any man and the fertilized eggs can be implanted in any woman. Theoretically the sperm, eggs and implantation site can all be from different people.

There is much debate in society over this technique. The Catholic church rejects this method to yield offspring for many reasons. The first reason is that the fertilized egg is considered to be a new individual; a new human life. Many fertilized eggs may be destroyed to obtain a viable pregnancy so human life is destroyed. Excess eggs are also usually destroyed again, destroying new human life. Another reason is that many eggs are usually inserted into the uterus and frequently more that one fertilized egg implants to result in more than one embryo. Sometimes three or four or even more embryos may implant. "Reductions" in the form of abortions must take place to remove the other embryos in excess of those desired. Again human life is destroyed. Again the Catholic church rejects this process as it does not involve sexual intercourse therefore it is not a natural process according to natural law to bear children.

There is some debate as to whether in vitro fertilization results in some sick children.

In vitro fertilization may allow some woman who otherwise might be considered sterile to bear children. Woman who were sterile from pelvic infections with fallopian tube occlusion may otherwise be able to bear children. Woman past the normal age of reproduction, with hormonal assistance can also bear children. While not a cure-all for infertility many infertile woman can bear children by this method.

There are many controversies with this method. People who do not have natural sexual attraction, who have fallen in love, and share the same philosophies in life can bear children. Woman can be egg donors and other men sperm donors without having to do with raising the offspring. Complete strangers can have children without the normal biologic and social backgrounds that are usually necessary for the upbringing on children. For this reason in vitro fertilization can present with the same problems as adoption. Parents unfamiliar with the genetic makeup of their children can be faced with problems of raising these children.

The author believe in what the Catholic church has stated-that in vitro fertilization should not be used in human or other populations as it violates the natural law and natural order of things. In vitro fertilization is not natural and occurs in the absence of natural love between man and woman and in the absence of sexual intercourse that results in fertilization. How in vitro fertilization effects the human is yet to be determined.

OF GENIUSES, IDIOTS, AND PLAIN OLD US

Many people think that all human life should be protected because one is never sure when a real genius might come to be born. Other people believe that not all life should be protected because idiots will be born among us. Some others believe that all life should be protected as some will be born just like us.

Geniuses are few and far between. Think of the genius of Leonardo Da Vinci, or Rembrandt, or Einstein, or Thomas Edison. These people have changed the lives of all of us. With wide scale abortion on the average of sixty million in the United States and one billion on the planet, many otherwise potentially bright and intelligent people were destroyed in their mothers wombs. As these were never to be replicated gene sequences that would have lived in never to be replicated environments, much has been lost to humanity. Never created art, science, music, and engineering have probably been lost forever. More importantly these people would have been in the image of God and a facet of God, sent to us in human form, that will forever be lost to human experience. The loss is unimaginable.

Again some people think that abortion should be legal to remove the idiots from among us. These idiots presumably consist of Mongolian idiots, Down syndrome babies, other biochemically and genetically challenged babies, and the rest. These babies are to costly, to sick, to retarded, and plain not like us so they should be destroyed. One asks how doctor's can ever cure these diseases unless babies are born that can be studied and treated. The argument intrinsically makes the point that unless people are not burdensome, are healthy, and can make a contribution to society that their life is valueless. Our values of some people is that unless they can help us they do not deserve to exist. Is it not enough that everyone who is born is a human being, with feelings and emotions that make them a part of the human race. Perhaps when we cannot find love in the way that we expect it that life is valueless to us. As a society we reject the different rather than appreciate it.

The saddest facet of the abortion debate is that many people who would be just plain old ordinary people get aborted in their mother's wombs. Do we hate ourselves so much that we would want to destroy our offspring. What is wrong with people who would be plumber's, or firemen, or nurses, or housecleaners. Unless someone is extraordinary, or beautiful, or rich, or famous they apparently do not have the right to carry a baby to term. The normal, the average, and the not so special should have just as much a right to bring offspring into the world.

A basic fact of the abortion debate is that we do not like ourselves, and do not like one another, so much in fact that we destroy ourselves and each other. The abortion industry has become our massive id, that causes the fullscale destruction of our next generations.

I wonder sometimes what god thinks of this whole abortion mentality. People who love babes will see their next generations wheras people who despise children will be destroyed.

EUTHANASIA

Euthanasia is when people are put to death before their natural death would occur as people intervene to cause death. It is most often perpetrated by the medical profession but can be performed by family members or others. It is sometimes referred to as mercy killing and when someone who wants to commit suicide is aided it is referred to as assisted suicide. In most cases it is voluntary. Some people who suffer pain or are sorely depressed or find life wearisome prefer euthanasia.

Quality of life is a concept propounded by the euthanasia proponents. If someone does not have a quality of life considered acceptable by the society then they should be relieved of life and put to death. This is different from the concept of life from conception to natural death. Life is terminated by human intervention. Pain and suffering might drive people to death by euthanasia. Pain and suffering may however be part of God's plan for their life to purify them and bring them to the realization of how much they depend on God in their lives.

Suicide is thought to be sinful and is in reality self murder. When it is assisted there is the murderer and the co-conspirators to murder. Suicide is a psychiatric phenomenon related to depression. Assisted suicide may interfere with proper treatment of depression. Human suffering caused by pain and depression are better treated by medication and medical therapy . The difference between euthanasia and natural death is a different as the concept of death by man's time and death by God's time. A time of life prior to natural death might allow one to put into perspective their lives and put their affairs in order- to ready themselves for eternity. Hastening death by artificial means may interfere with this process.

Euthanasia is a slippery slope in that when society or individuals choose to put themselves or others to death they devalue life. What may originally start off as a choice of when to die may progress to involuntary infliction of death on those who are considered unworthy to life or live "valueless" lives. People who are mentally retarded, sick, psychiatrically or mentally impaired might be put to death to improve the "health" of the society.

The whole argument revolves around the concept of death and man's ability to kill. Man may have idea's different from God's on how long a person should live and how they should die. With euthanasia man assumes a power of God- that is when a man or woman should die. Man become God.

People can choose suicide- who can stop them? When the medical profession or society assists them it again turns society and doctor's and nurses into murderers. There is a great difference between controlling someone's pain with medication and using high doses of pain medication to kill them.

Food and water, and basic life support are rights every person should have-even the sick. No one says its alright to artificially prolong life but man must not end it prematurely.

EUPHEMISMS

There are some euphemisms in the abortion culture which warrant discussion. The first of these is TOP or termination of pregnancy. This refers to an abortion, or the destruction of a human being. A pregnancy, or the intrauterine existence of an infant as it grows and matures is stopped and the infant killed so that the pregnancy stops. Another of the euphemisms associated with the abortion culture is POC or products of conception. This refers to the infant extracted from the womb-dead. Either whole or in pieces if the infant is ripped apart. These terms hide the gross reality that abortion murders a human being.

Therapeutic abortion suggests that the abortion is done for a valid reason to help save the life of the mother. In fact "therapeutic abortions" are rarely done to save the life of the mother, but only to preserve the psychological health of the mother-that is to say for the convenience of the mother.

With suction curettage, a plastic tube with a sharp surface for cutting is placed in the uterus. High suction is applied and the infant is torn apart by the high suction and sharp edge of the tube. With Saline abortion, high concentration salt water is placed in the uterus and the infant receives a massive chemical burn until it dies. With partial birth abortion, the baby is dragged out of the uterus with a forceps, a tube stuck into its brain which is sucked out, and the dead infant thus extracted.

An incomplete abortion is one where parts of the dead infant are still in the woman's body.

Choice is a word often given to the option of abortion. Women, fight politically for "choice" or the right to have an abortion. In fact choice is rarely the woman's be it that her boyfriend or husband coerces her, she is unable to pay the costs of bring a human being into the world, or the child is unwanted by society. "Unwanted" is another euphemism associated with the abortion culture. Unwanted by the mother or unwanted by the society, the baby is infant is aborted.

Maybe the woman's employer is not willing to pay the costs of having a job vacated temporarily, the baby is of the wrong race or ethnicity, for the culture, or for whatever reason the infant is destroyer.

The abortion pill refers to a chemical that kills the infant without surgery and expels the dead infant from the woman's body.

All the euphemisms that refer to abortion neglect the fact that an innocent human life is destroyed. All the euphemisms neglect to mention that a human life will not be born, not participate in the affairs of the world that occur under the sun. All the euphemisms obviate the fact that a human being has been murdered. All the terminology refers to a single act and neglects the fact of the high numbers of abortion that are completed and that these abortions may effectively result in genocide. All the terminology dismisses the value of the human person, denigrates life, and reduces the infant in the womb to tissue which can be discarded as if trash.

EMOTIONAL SCARS

Women who have had abortions are different psychologically and mentally.

Like miscarriage, there is sometimes a feeling of loss, in a woman who has had an abortion. Pregnancy and childbirth, a time that is supposed to be happy and joy filled becomes a time of sadness. It is the understanding of the author that women are prone to depression, crying spells, and misery after an abortion. Society does not allow women to acknowledge loss or grieve so there is also associated loneliness and isolation. The woman knows in her heart that something important and precious has been lost. These feelings may continue to the day the woman dies if these feelings are not dealt will in some constructive manner.

Woman can become callous after an abortion. They might think less of human life and go on to have other abortions, or be resentful when she sees another pregnant woman. Woman might become hardened to the value of human life and care less when somebody dies, or has an abortion. Women might lose their femininity or natural maternal instincts after an abortion. The constellation of altered feelings is so predictable it is often called the post abortion syndrome.

There is a slightly higher rate of suicide in woman who have had an abortion. When the realize the magnitude of their actions they can become so distraught as to cause themselves to take their own lives. It is a failure to reach out that often result in this unfortunate outcome. If women sough out psychiatric or psychological help this sad outcome might decrease. There are programs where women can express their feelings and help to cope such as project Rachel which is designed for post abortion syndrome.

Anger and rage may dominate the feelings of woman who have had abortions. Women might be angry with men or family members who have coerced them to have abortions. They may feel angry with God or themselves for putting themselves through such a procedure. Bitterness may also be felt by women who have had abortions.

When a woman who has had an abortion sees other women with young children how is she to feel? She might be envious of the other women's children and a sense of loss might be accentuated. A woman rendered sterile by an abortion procedure might be quite surprised when she tries to become pregnant and finds out she is unable to. Again anger and loss play a loss in the woman's feelings.

The abortion industry, psychologists, and psychiatrists rarely acknowledge a post abortion syndrome but have probably reaped tens of billions of dollars to treat women who have had abortions, more than fifty million. The drug industry for anxiety and depression has also benefited handsomely from the abortion business.

Shame can often follow women who have had abortions as the procedure has not lost all its stigma. Fear can also haunt women especially when their conscience and the possibility of hell for unforgiven sin way in. Perhaps confession to a priest can help.

THE ELDERLY

Another problem with abortion and the theory that those who are weak and vulnerable are also disposable is that we may one day be weak and vulnerable. The way we treat the weak and vulnerable may be the same way we are one day treated. When we respect life and there is a culture of life then there is a good chance that we may treated well when we become old and frail. The way we abuse the unborn infant may one day become the way we are abused. What goes around comes around.

Selfish people with bad values who disrespect life Values.

DUE PROCESS OF LAW

The United States Constitution states that no one should be deprived of life without due process of law. Unborn babies are not considered as alive because no-one has defined as when life begins so how can they receive due process of law. No-one has ever been able to find out if an aborted unborn infant wanted to live because they are killed before they can speak. Most living people are glad that they were given life and a chance to live. One can postulate that many if not all unborn babies killed by abortion would have preferred to live if given the chance. A life at conception act by congress would give definition of life to the unborn child and thus due process of law and protection by other provisions of the Constitution. The Declaration of Independence states that all men are endowed by their creator with certain unalienable rights among these the right to life. How then can we live in a society where the rights of the unborn infants are denied?

DISENFRANCHISED FATHERS

While the Roe V Wade decision gave mothers the exclusive right to destroy their unborn children, it also disenfranchised fathers of their unborn children. Fathers according to the judicial precedent have no say in whether their own unborn children can survive or not.

One might make the argument that the unborn child is the result of both man and woman so that both must have a say in whether a child is born or not, the government disagrees. It is the mother's life and body which are at issue. Since the man is not effected physically by pregnancy and does not put his life at risk for childbirth the man should have no say in the matter. From a genetic point of view the child represents a 50% share of his DNA.

The government argues that a couple should be left to the privacy of their own decision, and that a woman has the ultimate say in whether the unborn infant survives or not. The government puts the woman at the head of family decision making process not the couple or the man. A woman can thus deny a man a genetic inheritance with the family of man. The court might further assume that if a couple decide the destroy their child that both the man and the woman have agreed. There are no statistics to state how often this is true. Perhaps the man has severe disagreement with woman; he still has no say. The only alternative the man has is to break up with the woman.

Since the society and the government have so much control over the family- whether they can work, how much money the family makes, the resources of the family and other factors, it is the society and government who eventually decide how many children a couple have. Whether a woman uses birth control, sterilizes herself, or has an abortion is often determined by employers, family and friends. If a couple fits in with society and is well liked, they are more likely to afford more children.

Reproduction within a family, composed of husband and wife, is thus decided by the woman. Though their might be pre-agreement prior to marriage it is ultimately the woman who makes the decision as to number of children, if any. Some couples decide not to have children and this might result in higher rates of abortion if birth control fails.

In a marriage then men cannot force or coerce women to have children. Women must be charmed into having children. When population problems tax government resources, the government must make choices as to what couples reproduce and which ones do not or try to make laws as to how many children a couples can have.

Perhaps one day the government will figure out what makes people fall and love and have children. Effective population control can then be achieved by stopping people from falling in love and thus having children. Perhaps widespread sex with birth control will replace love for effective population control. Liberal abortion laws disenfranchise men from any role in human reproduction.

THOSE WITHOUT CHILDREN

It is always a wonder to see how those women without children and unable to bear them find children precious whereas those who are pregnant may not want children or those with children and pregnant might not want more. Some women want children desperately and are unable to even adopt whereas many pregnant women do not want children even to give them up for adoption.

In the bible there are several woman who wanted children yet did not conceive until fertility was granted to them by God. Abraham and Sarah desperately wanted a son of their own but Sarah was sterile and could not become pregnant. God did indeed promise them a son but they could not imagine that God would grant them one until they were way past the normal age of child bearing. There son Isaac was very precious to them and long wanted.

Samson's mother in the bible too was barren and unable to bear children. God however rendered her fertile and she was able to bear Samson. This child too was precious in the sight of the parents. God is able to render people fertile or infertile.

Man and woman today choose to render themselves fertile or infertile and there are many ways for a couple to do this. Perhaps man has chosen to take matters into their own hands rather than wait for God to accomplish this goal.

Hannah in the First book of Samuel in the bible is also a woman who was sterile. She became bitter in her infertility was mocked and teased for her barrenness. When she prayed to God in her sorrow God answered her prayer with a son. Samuel was instrumental in achieving God's plans through his life.

Then there is the Shunammite woman and Elisha. The Shunammite woman had no son in her old age and was essential sterile. Yet God through Elisha promised the woman that she would bear a son.

Lastly there is the story of Elizabeth in the book of Luke. Zechariah and Elizabeth ere both advanced in years and Elizabeth was barren. They were both righteous and blameless in the sight of God and God rewarded them with a son who was to become John the Baptist.

God, the author of life, can perform miracles in people's lives and grant them children. There were probably no doctors who were fertility experts in those days but simple prayer and proper living won them victory in a chain of life. How many times do people lose their fertility today by improper living and sexual excess. Then when they finally want children there are none to find.

Life is indeed precious in God's sight as it should be in all men's sight. Life in all its stages from conception to natural dearth should be protected . God, the author and finisher of life should be the only one to give or take life. Any attempt for man to attempt this role ends in disaster.

www.ingramcontent.com/pod-product-compliance
Lightning Source LLC
LaVergne TN
LVHW010551070526
838199LV00063BA/4938